D0044862

Sam the Man & the Rutabaga Plan

Also by Frances O'Roark Dowell

Anybody Shining
Chicken Boy
Dovey Coe
Falling In
The Second Life of Abigail Walker
Shooting the Moon
Ten Miles Past Normal
Trouble the Water
Where I'd Like to Be

The Secret Language of Girls Trilogy
The Secret Language of Girls
The Kind of Friends We Used to Be
The Sound of Your Voice, Only Really Far Away

From the Highly Scientific Notebooks of
Phineas L. MacGuire
Phineas L. MacGuire . . . Blasts Off!
Phineas L. MacGuire . . . Erupts!
Phineas L. MacGuire . . . Gets Cooking!
Phineas L. MacGuire . . . Gets Slimed!

The Sam the Man series
#1: *Sam the Man & the Chicken Plan*

SAM THE MAN 2:

SAM THE MAN

& the Rutabaga Plan

FRANCES O'ROARK DOWELL

Illustrated by **Amy June Bates**

A Caitlyn Dlouhy Book

Atheneum Books for Young Readers

atheneum New York London Toronto Sydney New Delhi

ATHENEUM BOOKS FOR YOUNG READERS
An imprint of Simon & Schuster Children's Publishing Division
1230 Avenue of the Americas, New York, New York 10020

This book is a work of fiction. Any references to historical events, real people, or real places are used fictitiously. Other names, characters, places, and events are products of the author's imagination, and any resemblance to actual events or places or persons, living or dead, is entirely coincidental.

ATHENEUM BOOKS FOR YOUNG READERS is a registered trademark of Simon & Schuster, Inc. Atheneum logo is a trademark of Simon & Schuster, Inc.
For information about special discounts for bulk purchases, please contact Simon & Schuster Special Sales at 1-866-506-1949 or business@simonandschuster.com.
The Simon & Schuster Speakers Bureau can bring authors to your live event. For more information or to book an event, contact the Simon & Schuster Speakers Bureau at 1-866-248-3049 or visit our website at www.simonspeakers.com.
Book design by Sonia Chaghatzbanian and Irene Metaxatos
The text for this book was set in New Century Schoolbook LT Std.
The illustrations for this book are rendered in pencil.
Manufactured in the United States of America
0117 FFG
First Edition
10   9   8   7   6   5   4   3   2   1
CIP data for this book is available from the Library of Congress.
ISBN 978-1-4814-4069-1
ISBN 978-1-4814-4071-4 (eBook)

For Jeff Burch,
wonderful friend, extraordinary teacher
—F. O. D.

For Rosebuds and rutabagas
—A. J. B.

Chapter One

Welcome to Your Vegetable

Sam Graham was not a vegetable man.

"Two cups a day, Sam," his mom liked to say. "That's all it takes to be healthy."

"That's two cups of important vitamins and minerals, Sam the Man," his dad always added.

"It's two cups of stuff that probably still has dirt on it even though Mom washed it," his sister, Annabelle, usually pointed out.

"I'll eat extra grapes," Sam told his mom whenever she tried to make him eat steamed broccoli or spinach salad. "And three bananas a day."

"Fruit is good," his mom would say. "But you need vegetables, too."

Vegetables, in Sam's opinion, were overrated. They were either too crunchy or too slimy. Most of them looked weird. Especially broccoli. Sam thought broccoli looked unnatural, like it was trying to be a tree but had forgotten to read the instruction manual.

He didn't even want to think about asparagus. You could have nightmares about asparagus.

So when his second-grade teacher, Mr. Pell, announced they were going to start a new science unit first thing Monday morning, and that that unit would be all about vegetables, Sam was glad he had an appointment to get his teeth cleaned.

That was another thing about broccoli—it got stuck in your teeth, and you wouldn't even know it until you looked in the mirror. Sam bet his dentist, Dr. Jenny, hated broccoli as much as he did.

"Actually, Sam, broccoli is a good source of calcium, and calcium is good for your teeth and bones," Dr. Jenny told him that Monday morning. She was poking at his gums with a dental pick. "If you floss after you eat, you don't have to worry about broccoli in your teeth, now do you?"

Sam guessed not. "But what if I forget to floss?" he asked. "Because sometimes I do, and then there's all that broccoli stuck in there. It's gross."

Dr. Jenny raised her eyebrow. "Do you floss every day?"

"Most of the time," Sam said.

"Almost all of the time?" Dr. Jenny asked.

"Almost most of some of the time," Sam said.

Sam left Dr. Jenny's office with four trial-sized packs of dental floss and a booklet called *Flossing: How to Be Your Teeth's Best Friend!*

Sam didn't know his teeth even had friends.

"The point is, you need to floss," his mom said as she signed him in at the front office when they got to school. "Your plaque score was a five!"

"But no cavities!" Sam said. He smiled as big as he could, so his mom could see all his perfect teeth.

Walking down the hall to his classroom, Sam felt happy that he had missed science, even if his plaque score was five. He would rather have plaque than learn about vegetables any day.

"Good morning, Sam!" Mr. Pell greeted him when Sam walked into Room 11. "I hope you're ready to learn about the wonderful world of vegetables. For the next two weeks, you and a very special vegetable are going to get to know each other. You're going to study your vegetable, write about your vegetable, and teach us a thing or two about your vegetable."

"What do you mean, *my* vegetable?" Sam asked.

The other kids started to giggle. That's

when Sam noticed that everyone had a vegetable on his or her desk.

Gavin had a carrot.

Will had a head of cabbage.

Rashid had a tiny pumpkin.

Emily had a green bean.

Marja had an eggplant.

There was something on Sam's desk too, only he didn't know what it was.

It was the size of a softball.

It was round, but not perfectly round.

One half was purple, and the other half was a dirty yellow.

There was a weird brown thing sticking out of the top like a little tree stump.

"What is *that*?" Sam asked.

"It's a rutabaga!" Will yelled. Everybody started laughing, and Gavin laughed so hard he fell out of his seat.

Mr. Pell came over to Sam's desk. "Sam," he said, "I'd like to introduce you to your vegetable. I think the two of you are about to become very good friends."

Chapter Two

Sam Graham the Rutabaga Man

Sam was now sorry he'd had his teeth cleaned.

In first period, while Dr. Jenny was poking at Sam's gums, everyone else was choosing a vegetable. They had all pulled numbers from a paper bag, and the person who picked 1 (Emily) got to choose first, and the person who picked 2 (Hutch) got to choose second, and so on.

Because Sam hadn't been there, he got

last pick, which is how he got stuck with a rutabaga for the next two weeks. And now for homework he had to write a one-page letter from his rutabaga's point of view.

Sam was pretty sure vegetables didn't have a point of view.

But even if some vegetables *did* have a point of view, like maybe carrots or peas, he was positive that rutabagas didn't. A carrot might say, *My favorite color is orange*, and that would make sense. *It scares me when I roll under the table,* a pea might tell you, and you'd understand.

But a rutabaga? What would a rutabaga have to say about anything?

"It probably has a lot of opinions about dirt," Sam's neighbor Mr. Stockfish said after school that day. Mr. Stockfish and Sam were feeding chickens in the coop behind Mrs. Kerner's house. Sam had two after-school jobs: walking Mr. Stockfish and taking care of chickens. He was responsible for eight chickens in all, including his own chicken, Helga, who laid blue eggs, and Mr. Stockfish's chicken, Leroy, who laid regular white eggs.

Sam poured two cups of grain into the chickens' feeder. "Why would a rutabaga have an opinion on dirt?" he asked.

"Because it's a root vegetable," Mr. Stockfish said. "It does all its growing underground."

"So, it lives in the dark until somebody eats it? That's its whole life?"

"What's so bad about that?" Mr. Stockfish asked. He was sitting in a lawn chair. He called himself the chicken

supervisor, which meant Sam did the work while Mr. Stockfish watched.

"It's boring! And you're surrounded by dirt all the time!"

"What are they teaching at that school of yours?" Mr. Stockfish asked. "Dirt is one of the most interesting things in the world. Did you know there are more than ten thousand different kinds of bacteria in one teaspoon of soil?"

"That makes dirt sound very unhealthy," Sam said.

Mr. Stockfish snorted and shook his head.

"There's a lot you don't know about bacteria, Sam," he said. "Bacteria makes the world go 'round."

"Well, I wish bacteria was a vegetable, then," Sam said. "It sounds like it would be a much better project than a rutabaga."

After Sam gave the chickens their water, he plopped in the lawn chair next to Mr. Stockfish. He wondered if chickens ate rutabagas. Maybe that's what his rutabaga's letter could be about. *Dear Mom, Today I got eaten by eight chickens. Now I'm dead. Bye.*

Sam liked that idea. If his rutabaga got eaten by chickens, then Mr. Pell would have to give him another vegetable. Maybe he'd get a banana pepper next time. Sam could think of lots of things a banana pepper might write a letter about. *Dear Mom, Today I took a ride in a pizza box to a boy named Sam's house. . . .*

"Chickens don't eat rutabagas," Mr. Stockfish said when Sam told him his plan. "What are you, crazy?"

13

Sam decided to look it up when he got home. But first he would have to get his mom's permission to use her computer.

"I'm working," his mom said when he knocked on her office door. Sam's mom worked at home some days and at an office across town the other days. When she worked at home, Sam was only supposed to knock on her door if he had an emergency situation.

Sam was pretty sure having to do a

rutabaga project counted as an emergency situation.

"You want to feed your rutabaga to the chickens so you can do another vegetable?" his mom said when Sam explained why he needed to go on the Internet. "Do you think that's fair?"

"To the rutabaga or the chickens?" Sam asked.

"I mean, to, well, the other kids, I guess," his mom said. She sounded like she wasn't sure what she meant. "What if everyone fed their vegetables to chickens in order to get a new one?"

"But I'm the only person in my class with a chicken," Sam said. "A lot of people have dogs, but I don't think dogs like vegetables."

His mother sighed. "Sorry, Sam. You're

stuck with your rutabaga. If the chickens ate the one you have now, we'd just go to the store and buy another one. So you better get started on your letter."

Sam went to his room, sat down at his desk, and opened his science notebook. He picked up his pencil. He put his pencil down. He picked it up again and chewed on the end, and then he wondered if he had yellow pencil bits in his teeth.

Maybe I should floss, Sam thought. Yes, he should floss. He put his pencil down.

The rutabaga letter would have to wait.

Chapter Three

Or Are You a Turnip?

The problem was, Sam didn't know the first thing about rutabagas.

"I'll do a search on my phone," Annabelle said at the dinner table that night. "I'm sure there are lots of interesting facts to be found."

"No phones at the table," their mom said.

"Family time is phone-free time," added their dad.

"But this is important," Annabelle said. "This is for school."

Their parents both shook their heads no. Annabelle looked at Sam. "Meet me in the family room after dinner," she said.

After dinner, Sam and Annabelle sat on the couch and looked up facts about rutabagas. Maybe rutabagas were first eaten by Vikings, Sam thought, or were used in Native American games. Maybe rutabagas were the world's first lacrosse balls.

"Well, this is interesting," Annabelle said, peering into her phone.

"What?" Sam asked, feeling a little bit excited. Maybe there was good news about rutabagas after all!

"What's interesting about rutabagas is there is absolutely nothing interesting

about rutabagas," Annabelle reported. She handed the phone to Sam. "See for yourself."

Sam scrolled down, and he scrolled up. There were entries for articles like "Why

You Should Give Rutabagas a Chance" and "Rutabagas: They're Not So Bad."

"In Sweden they call rutabagas 'turnips,'" Sam read to Annabelle. "And they are often roasted. I wonder what's the difference between a rutabaga and a turnip?"

"I wonder how you say 'turnip' in Swedish," Annabelle said.

"I could look it up," Sam said.

"You could," said Annabelle. "Except I need my phone back, and you need to write your letter."

Sam went upstairs. He climbed up onto his bed and looked at his rutabaga. "Hello, turnip," he said, feeling mean. "How does it feel to know that you're the most boring vegetable on Earth?"

Then Sam felt bad. His rutabaga couldn't help being boring. Besides, it was half purple. That was sort of not boring, Sam guessed.

Sam went over to his desk. He took a seat and picked up his partly chewed pencil. He wrote:

Dear Students of Room 11,

My name is Rudy the

Rutabaga. I am half purple.

Other things that are purple

are grapes that are not green

and ~~patoonas patunyas~~

purple flowers. Also, lollipops

and grape soda. The other

half of me is yellow. My skin

is smooth. If you lost your

ball on the playground, you

could throw me. It wouldn't

even matter if you dropped

me, because I am not a

pumpkin. I won't smash.

Sam stopped writing because he guessed that was all he had to say. He had two thoughts. One, he wished he'd gotten a pumpkin for his vegetable. Then he could write his letter about being a Halloween pumpkin and which costumes he thought were the scariest and which ones were dumb.

His second thought was that his rutabaga was round like a pumpkin. It was even bigger than some of the very small pumpkins Sam had seen at the grocery store.

"I think I would like you better if you had a face," Sam told his rutabaga.

Sam crossed the hallway to Annabelle's room and knocked on her door.

"Could you help me give my rutabaga a face?" he asked when she answered.

Annabelle opened up her desk drawer and pulled out a thick black marker. "Should it be a happy face or a sad face?"

"I think it should be a medium happy face," Sam said. "Like it's listening to you talk and likes what you're saying."

Annabelle nodded. "That's exactly the right kind of face for a rutabaga," she said.

"I think so too," Sam said.

Chapter Four

House of Dirt

Now that his rutabaga had a face, Sam felt they were more like friends than just a boy and his vegetable.

When he put Rudy in his backpack the next morning, he said, "You'll like it in there. It's dark and pretty dirty."

Rudy smiled up at him. He seemed to like what Sam was saying.

It was easier to have happy feelings

about a rutabaga when it had a face, Sam thought.

As always, he sat next to Gavin on the bus. Gavin had a box in his lap. "This is my carrot's house," Gavin told Sam. "It doesn't have a bathroom, though. Do you think that's a problem?"

"Do carrots poop?" Sam asked.

"I think maybe their peels are poop," Gavin said. "But I'm not positive."

Then Gavin got very quiet. He looked left. He looked right. Then he leaned in close to Sam's ear and said, "The carrot in the box is not actually the carrot Mr. Pell gave me yesterday."

"Where's that carrot?" Sam asked.

Gavin's cheeks turned red. "I ate it," he said. "I got hungry doing my spelling homework."

"I guess I'm lucky, then," Sam said. "It's hard to snack on a rutabaga."

He pulled Rudy out of his backpack and showed Gavin. "He might be the only smiling rutabaga on the planet," Sam said proudly.

"You're so lucky to have a vegetable with a face!" Gavin said. "And one that's hard to eat, too. I wished I'd picked a rutabaga."

"But at least you have a vegetable that rabbits like," Sam said, trying to be nice. "Maybe part of your project could be about all the animals that eat carrots. Maybe you could bring a horse to school for a demonstration."

Gavin's eyes lit up. "My sister has a friend whose cousin has a horse!"

Sam didn't think there were any

animals that ate rutabagas. From what he'd read so far, most humans didn't eat them either.

Sam sighed. He was glad Rudy had a face, but he was still boring.

When Sam got to Room 11, he saw that a lot of the vegetables had their own houses. Emily's green bean lived in a pencil box, and Rashid's tiny pumpkin lived in a square plastic container. Rashid had added some grass and candy corn for decoration.

Sam thought maybe his rutabaga would like his own house instead of living in Sam's backpack. But he didn't think Rudy would like to spend all day in a pencil box or a plastic container, even one that had candy corn for decorations. What Sam needed for Rudy was a box of dirt.

A box of really good dirt.

※   ※   ※

"You need to start a compost pile," Mr. Stockfish told him that afternoon when they were walking home after taking care of the chickens. "That way, you'll have the best dirt in town."

"What's a compost pile?" Sam asked.

"It's where you mix leaves and vegetable scraps and manure all together, add some water, and cook it," Mr. Stockfish said.

"In an oven?" Sam asked, alarmed. He doubted his mom would think this was a good idea.

"No," Mr. Stockfish said. "You can either get a compost bin or you can just pile scraps in your backyard and mix it around every couple of days. The pile heats up as everything rots, and after a while it turns into dirt. But remember—

no meat or dairy products. They attract animals."

"What's manure again?" Sam asked.

"Animal poop," Mr. Stockfish answered. "Chicken poop is great for compost."

Sam wrinkled his nose. He found it very hard to believe that chicken poop was good for anything. Still, if it would help Rudy, he guessed he should give a compost pile a try.

"I need to start a pile of chicken manure and vegetable scraps in the backyard," Sam announced that night at dinner. "It's for school."

"Not going to happen, Sam the Man," his dad said.

"It sounds unsanitary," his mom said.

"Not to mention unappetizing," Annabelle said.

"But it's for a school," Sam repeated. "I'm making a compost pile. It's for *science*."

Usually, if he said he was doing something for science, his parents gave him permission right away. Science was like a magic word to them.

"So why don't you start a pile of chicken manure and vegetable scraps at school?" Annabelle asked.

"It's a personal science project," Sam said. "It's not for the whole class."

"It's for your rutabaga, isn't it?" Annabelle asked.

"My rutabaga needs the best dirt nature can offer," Sam said.

"Sam the Man, you know your rutabaga has stopped growing, right?" Sam's dad said.

"Yes, but I want it to have a happy home," Sam said. "For *science*."

"What do you do with the manure from Mrs. Kerner's chicken coop?" his mom asked.

"I clean it out of the coop, and then I—"

"And then you what?" his mom asked.

"I throw it in a pile near the back of her yard."

"Sounds like you already have a chicken manure pile, Sam the Man," his dad said. "All you need to do is add leaves and vegetable scraps. I'm sure Mrs. Kerner won't mind."

Wow, Sam thought, that was easy.

Now all he had to do was ask Mrs. Kerner if he could add things to her pile of chicken poop, like carrot peels and bread crusts and potato skins.

"I'm going to make you some great dirt," Sam told Rudy that night before he turned his bedroom light out. "You're going to be the happiest rutabaga in the world."

Rudy smiled at him, and Sam zipped up his backpack.

"Good night," Sam said.

Rudy didn't say good night back. Sam guessed he was already asleep, and then Sam remembered that rutabagas didn't talk.

Or maybe Sam just didn't understand their language.

Yet.

Chapter Five

Sam the Man and the Compost Business Plan

The next morning Sam emptied out his trash can onto his bedroom floor and then took it downstairs.

"This is my scrap-collecting bin," he told his mom. "So that I can grow dirt. I'll need all your eggshells and vegetable scraps. No meat or dairy products, please."

"You know, Sam, you could probably make a deal with some of our neighbors to collect their vegetable scraps too," his mom said. "You could start another business."

"A scrap-collecting business?"

"A compost business. People like to use compost in their vegetable gardens. It has lots of good microbes and nutrients in it. You could collect their scraps, add them to your compost pile, and then give them some of the compost when it's done."

"I'd need a bigger trash can."

"I'm sure we have a bucket or two around here you could use," Sam's mom said. "And we can dig out your old wagon from the garage. You could use it when you're collecting scraps."

Sam told Gavin about his new business plan on the bus ride to school. "Rudy will have the best dirt of any rutabaga ever," he said.

"You know he's done growing, right?" Gavin asked.

"I know," said Sam.

"So just how long do you plan to keep Rudy? I mean, after we're done with our vegetable unit in science?"

Sam shrugged. "Forever, I guess."

"I don't think vegetables last forever," Gavin said. "By the time you have really good dirt from your compost pile, Rudy might be, well—"

"Well, what?" Sam asked, even though he wasn't sure he wanted to hear the answer.

"Have you ever looked in the vegetable bin of your fridge?" Gavin asked. "You know, when it hasn't been cleaned out in a long time?"

Sam nodded.

"So you know stuff gets kind of brown and mushy?"

Sam looked down at his lap. He knew.

"You could just eat him," Gavin said. "I mean, when we're done with the unit. Emily said her mom told her she had to eat her green bean by tonight or throw it away."

Sam was shocked. "I don't eat my friends," he told Gavin.

"You would if they were carrots," Gavin said.

At school, Sam looked around Mr. Pell's classroom and wondered if everyone was planning to eat their vegetables. Was Caitlyn going to bake her potato and eat it with sour cream and butter? Was Will going to chop up his cabbage into coleslaw? Was Rashid going to make pumpkin pie?

"Don't worry, Rudy," he whispered into his backpack. "You're safe."

But for how long?

That afternoon, Sam told Mr. Stockfish about his new business plan.

"How are you going to make money doing that?" Mr. Stockfish asked. He was holding Leroy in his lap and scratching her head.

"I'm not doing it for the money," Sam explained. "I'm doing it for the dirt."

"That's not much of a business plan," Mr. Stockfish said. "But okay."

"'Okay' what?" Sam asked.

"Okay, I'll help. When we finish with the chickens, we can walk down the street and knock on doors."

Sam wasn't sure he wanted Mr.

Stockfish to help. Mr. Stockfish was grumpy. Sam didn't think regular people liked to do business with grumpy people.

"Maybe I should go up to the door by myself," Sam said when they reached the first house. "So the people will see me as a real businessperson and not just some little kid who needs a grown-up's help."

"I suppose you have a point," Mr. Stockfish replied. "But call me if you need to do any wheeling and dealing."

Sam didn't know who lived in the house, but he could see that whoever did liked to garden. There were four rose-bushes in the front yard and a potted plant on the steps.

A woman with white hair and glasses hanging from a chain around her neck answered the door. "Are you selling popcorn?" she asked when she saw Sam.

"No," Sam said.

"Candy? Raffle tickets? Band T-shirts? Because I don't need any of those things. And I'm allergic to nuts."

"I'm not here to sell you anything," Sam said. He was starting to wish they had skipped this house, even if there were four rosebushes in the yard and a potted plant on the steps.

"I'm here because I have a compost business," Sam explained. "If you give me your vegetable scraps, I'll put them in my compost pile, and then I'll give you some of the compost when it's cooked."

"How much?" the woman asked. She sounded suspicious.

"How much what?" Sam asked. "How much compost?"

"How much are you going to charge me for the compost you make out of my vegetable scraps?"

"Nothing," Sam said.

"Aw, make her pay something!" Mr. Stockfish called from the sidewalk. "At least a dollar!"

"Nothing," Sam repeated. "I need good dirt, and your vegetable scraps would help me make it."

"Do you have a garden?" the woman asked. "Compost is excellent for growing flowers."

"I have a rutabaga," Sam said.

"You're growing rutabagas?" the woman asked. She sounded excited, like growing rutabagas was one of the best things a second-grade boy could do with his spare time.

"No, it's grown already," Sam explained. "I have it at home in my backpack."

"You know it won't grow anymore, right?" the woman asked. "Even if you put it back into the dirt?"

"I know," Sam said with a sigh.

The woman was quiet for a minute. She had a look on her face that seemed to say, I am the sort of person who thinks very carefully before I act.

Finally she said, "Okay, count me in. My name is Stella Montgomery. You can collect my scraps every afternoon. I'll keep them in a bucket."

"No meat or dairy, please," Sam said. "Meat and dairy attract pests."

"I wasn't born yesterday, young man," Stella Montgomery said, and then went back inside.

Sam knocked on five more doors. No one was home at three of the houses, but at the other two houses, the people said Sam could collect the scraps and keep the compost.

After five houses, Sam was ready to go home. So was Mr. Stockfish.

"Did you ask Mrs. Kerner about the compost pile?" Mr. Stockfish asked when Sam dropped him off at his front door.

Sam had not asked Mrs. Kerner. One, Mrs. Kerner had not been home that afternoon. Two, he was afraid she would say no. If he didn't ask her, she couldn't tell him it wasn't okay.

"You need to ask her, Sam," Mr. Stockfish said. "It's her yard."

"I'm going to surprise her," Sam said. "I think she has a birthday coming up."

"You're going to surprise her with a compost pile for her birthday?" Mr. Stockfish asked. He sounded like he didn't think this was a very good idea.

"Yes," Sam said, pleased that he'd thought of it. "I'm pretty sure it's what she's always wanted."

Chapter Six

The Birthday Party Plan

"I have *never* wanted a compost pile in my backyard for my birthday," Mrs. Kerner said the next day. "What I want is a 1965 Ford Mustang convertible. A red one."

"I don't think I can afford that," Sam said.

Sam's plan had been to surprise Mrs. Kerner on her birthday with a wonderful compost pile. But his mom had said this was not the best plan.

"People like to be surprised with flowers and jewelry, Sam," she'd said. "They do not like to be surprised by rotten vegetables and moldy bread crusts."

So Sam had to promise he would tell Mrs. Kerner what he had planned for her birthday. As it turned out, her birthday was only two weeks away. Unfortunately, she did not want a compost pile for a present.

"There are any number of things I'd like," Mrs. Kerner told Sam. They were sitting in her kitchen. Mrs. Kerner was drinking peppermint tea, and Sam was drinking milk and eating a lemon cookie with lemon cream icing. When he looked out the window he could see Mr. Stockfish in the backyard talking to Leroy.

"I would like a new pair of bowling shoes, for instance," Mrs. Kerner continued. "I

49

would like an ice-cream maker. I have always wanted a pony. But a compost pile? A compost pile has never been on my list."

Sam was disappointed. Now he would have to ask Mrs. Kerner's permission to make a compost pile in her backyard. This was not as fun as giving it to her as a surprise. Also, now she could say no.

"One thing I would like this year is a party," Mrs. Kerner said. "With games."

"What kind of games?" Sam asked. "Like tag and dodgeball?"

"No," Mrs. Kerner said. "I would like to play charades and Authors and bingo."

"We could play the game called 'Let's

Build a Compost Pile'!" Sam suggested. "It's really fun."

"Sam, you are obsessed with compost," Mrs. Kerner said. "Would you care to explain why?"

Sam told Mrs. Kerner about Rudy the Rutabaga and how he wanted to make Rudy a nice place to live, and yes, he knew Rudy wasn't going to grow anymore, but Rudy still might like some nice dirt to spend his time in.

"And compost makes the best kind of dirt, am I right?" Mrs. Kerner said.

"Yes," Sam said. "I think Rudy deserves really good dirt."

"Sam, let's make a deal," Mrs. Kerner said. "If you help me plan a birthday party, I will help you compost. I don't want a pile, though. Raccoons will get into it, and then they'll eat our chickens."

"So what will we do?" Sam asked.

"We'll get posts and chicken wire and then build a proper compost bin. But can I ask you one thing?"

Sam nodded.

"Do you know you can go to a garden store and buy a bag of compost?"

Sam did not know that. Maybe that's what he should do, he thought. He had money saved up from his jobs, so he could probably afford a bag of compost. It would be faster than waiting for the vegetable scraps and bread crusts and chicken manure to heat up and rot and turn into dirt.

The fact was, Sam didn't know how much time Rudy had before he started getting mushy and brown.

"Maybe I could do both," Sam said. "Maybe I could buy some compost and also make some compost."

"That's a good plan, Sam," Mrs. Kerner said. "So you'll help me with my birthday party?"

"I'll help," Sam said. "Do you want a cake?"

"I would prefer cupcakes," Mrs. Kerner said. "With sprinkles."

"I like sprinkles too," said Sam. "Especially red ones on top of vanilla frosting."

"Those are the most festive kind," Mrs. Kerner agreed. "Now, who should we invite to my party?"

"Who do you want to invite?" Sam asked.

"You and Mr. Stockfish of course," Mrs. Kerner said.

"And I would like to invite the mail carrier, Francine, and also Curtis, who bags my groceries at the Shop 'n' Save Grocery."

"That's it?" Sam asked. He didn't think that seemed like very many people.

Mrs. Kerner was quiet for a minute. Then she said, "That's it."

Sam drank the rest of his milk and finished his cookie. "I should go feed the chickens," he said. For some reason, he felt sort of sad, and he thought seeing the chickens would cheer him up.

Mrs. Kerner stood up. "Yes, and I should—do something."

But Mrs. Kerner didn't do anything. She just kept standing there.

"Maybe you could come out and talk to Mr. Stockfish," Sam said. "That way he won't get lonely while I'm taking care of the chickens."

"I think that's a good idea, Sam," Mrs. Kerner said. "I would hate for Mr. Stockfish to get lonely."

When they got to the backyard, Mr. Stockfish was sitting in his usual lawn chair. Leroy perched in his lap.

"You sit there, Mrs. Kerner," Sam said, pointing to the chair next to Mr. Stockfish. "I'm going to clean out the coop."

"Did it ever occur to you that Leroy is an odd name for a girl?" Sam heard Mrs. Kerner ask Mr. Stockfish, who growled but didn't actually answer the question.

Sam thought he'd better hurry. He wasn't sure Mrs. Kerner and Mr. Stockfish should be left alone together for very long.

Sam crawled into the chicken coop.

The chickens came running, clucking and looking like they were happy to see him. They knew Sam was the person who brought them their food. He was like a rock star to them.

"I have to clean out your mess first," Sam told the chickens. To clean the coop he had to carry out the dirty straw from the ground and the laying boxes and put it in a wheelbarrow that he wheeled to the way back part of the backyard. After that, he shoveled up the chicken manure and put that in the wheelbarrow and wheeled it over to the same place he'd put the dirty straw.

He wondered what the bottom of the pile of manure and dirty straw looked like. He decided to poke at it with a stick.

A long stick.

Sam found a stick and poked at the straw. The bottom of the pile was black. It was goopy. Was it . . . turning into dirt?

If it was, then making dirt was a much slimier process than Sam had realized.

Sam turned around to ask Mr. Stockfish to come over and take a look. He wanted to know if this was really compost or something gross they should call the garbage men to come and haul away.

But Mr. Stockfish was busy talking to Mrs. Kerner, who now was holding Queen Bee, the head chicken, in her lap. Mr. Stockfish was pointing at the comb on top of Leroy's head.

Mrs. Kerner was laughing.

Mr. Stockfish was not frowning.

Sam decided his question could wait.

Chapter Seven

Every Vegetable Has a Story

" **W** ould you like to come to a birthday party in two weeks?" Sam asked Gavin on the bus the next day.

"Who's it for?" Gavin asked.

"My neighbor Mrs. Kerner," Sam said.

"The one whose chickens you take care of?" Gavin asked.

"Yes," Sam said. He wanted to point out that when he went to Mrs. Kerner's, he was taking care of his own chicken too, not to mention Mr. Stockfish's chicken, Leroy. But sometimes with Gavin it was better to keep your answers simple.

"Can we play with the chickens at the party?" Gavin asked.

"Chickens are not toys," Sam said. "But there will be games and cupcakes with vanilla icing and red sprinkles."

"Those are the best kind," Gavin said. "Do I need to bring a present?"

"Of course," Sam said.

"I'll think of something good," Gavin promised. "Maybe I'll bring her some carrots."

Gavin's mom had bought a two-pound bag of carrots at the grocery store, and now Gavin brought a new carrot in to school every day. So far Mr. Pell had not caught on, though he had mentioned the day before that Gavin's carrot had stayed remarkably fresh. "Some of you might not be as lucky as Gavin," he'd told the class. "In fact, I've heard from a few of your parents that your vegetables are starting to droop. It's okay if you want to leave them at home in the fridge."

"Don't worry," Sam had whispered to Rudy, who was snuggled down inside his backpack. "I'm keeping you right by my side."

Their latest vegetable assignment was to write a vegetable story. Everyone had to write a story about their vegetable that could be true, or at least mostly true. So if your vegetable was a cauliflower, you could have your cauliflower talk, but it had to talk about things that actually happened to cauliflowers. Your cauliflower could talk about getting rained on and eaten by worms, but it couldn't describe going to the state fair and eating a fried candy bar.

Emily Early was the first one to read her story. She walked to the front of the classroom with her pencil box. When she opened the box, she took out a picture of a green bean. "This is my bean before I ate it," she said, showing everyone the picture. "He was delicious. Now I'm going to tell you the story of my green bean's life, beginning with his days as a seed and ending with how he got digested inside of me."

Gavin leaned over to Sam and whispered, "This could be supergross."

"I hope so," said Sam.

After Emily was done, Marja took up her eggplant. "I have some shocking news.

An eggplant is really a fruit!" She turned to Mr. Pell. "Did you know that?"

Mr. Pell nodded. "So are tomatoes and bell peppers. But most people think of them as vegetables."

"Most people are wrong," Marja said. "A fruit has seeds on the inside. Vegetables don't."

When Will brought up his cabbage, he asked Mr. Pell, "Is a cabbage a fruit or a vegetable? Because it's sort of the same size as one of those little watermelons, so maybe it's a fruit."

That's when Mr. Pell explained that fruits were the flowering part of plants that contained seeds. Vegetables were the rest of the plant—the leaves, roots, stems, and in the case of broccoli and cauliflower, the flower buds.

"I'm still confused," Will said.

Mr. Pell laughed. "It's confusing," he admitted. "Mainly, we divide fruits and vegetables along the lines of sweet and unsweet."

"You could have told us the truth about vegetables," Emily said from her seat. She sounded mad. "We're not little kids."

"You're right," Mr. Pell agreed. "I promise to be honest with you from now on."

When it was Sam's turn, he carried up his backpack to the front of the room. He opened it so that everyone could see Rudy inside. Some of the kids waved at Rudy. Probably because he was smiling, Sam thought.

"Today I am going to tell you the story of Rudy and dirt," Sam said, and a few of the boys clapped. Dirt was a very popular topic with the second-grade boys at Sam's

school. "Rutabagas are root vegetables, which means they spend most of their lives underground. They like dirt a lot."

Sam told his classmates about how vegetables got important vitamins and minerals from dirt. Dirt helped vegetables get the water and oxygen they needed to live and grow. It gave root vegetables a nice habitat. Before he met Sam, dirt had been Rudy's best friend, Sam explained. That was why Sam was going to make a compost bin, so that Rudy could live in great dirt all his life.

"That was more a report than a story," Emily said when Sam was done.

Mr. Pell said, "You know your rutabaga is done growing, right?"

"I know," said Sam. "I've known that all week."

Sam walked back to his desk. He wondered if Emily had been right. He'd told everyone a lot of interesting facts, but that wasn't the same thing as telling a story. In a story, someone had to be in trouble or have a problem, and then they had to figure out how to get out of trouble or solve their problem. Sometimes in stories, a person wanted something really, really bad, but stuff kept getting in the way.

So what did Rudy want, Sam wondered? What was Rudy's problem he needed to solve?

Rashid walked to the front of the classroom carrying the plastic container that held his tiny pumpkin. He looked sad, as though he had bad news.

"My mom says she thinks my pumpkin was pretty old when I got it on Monday,"

Rashid said. "And also, maybe I should have kept my pumpkin in a cool place. So here's the story about how my pumpkin is getting rotten spots and why I have to throw it away today or else my mom's going to throw it away for me."

Rashid opened up the plastic container. All of a sudden a pumpkin-y smell filled the room. It wasn't a bad smell, Sam thought, but it wasn't a good smell, either. It was an old mushy pumpkin smell.

Sam opened up his backpack again and

pulled out Rudy. Rudy was not mushy or soft or stinky. He was exactly the same as he'd been on Monday. But one day he could be just like Rashid's tiny pumpkin if he wasn't careful.

That was Rudy's problem! He was a vegetable, and vegetables get rotten after a while. Unless . . . unless what? What could Rudy do to keep from getting soft and stinky?

Sam opened his science notebook and started writing. *Once there was a ruta-baga named Rudy, who wanted to live a long, long time. But how?*

Sam leaned back in his seat. The problem was, he had no idea how. But there must be a way to find out. Sam needed to do some research. He knew just the person to ask for help.

69

Chapter Eight

Rudy, the Angry Rutabaga

"You want to use my phone for what?" Annabelle asked at dinner that night.

"Research," Sam said. "I need to do research for a story I'm writing about Rudy."

"Who's Rudy?" Sam's dad asked. "Is he a new friend of yours?"

"He's my rutabaga," Sam said. "Haven't you been paying attention?"

"Sorry, Sam the Man," his dad said.

"It's been a busy week at work."

"My question is this," Sam said, turning to Annabelle, who was probably the only person at the table who could help him. "What can I do to stop Rudy from getting brown and mushy?"

"Not a dinner table discussion, Sam," his mom said.

"That's a little bit on the disgusting side, Sam the Man," his dad added.

"Eat him," Annabelle said.

"I can't eat him and keep him," Sam said.

"You can't keep him and keep him," Annabelle said. "Vegetables are not meant to live forever. They're part of nature, just like me and you."

"But I'm going to live forever," Sam said. "I think everyone will in the future."

71

"You know what I think you should do?" Annabelle asked. "Put Rudy in your compost bin."

"But I'm building a compost bin to make dirt for Rudy."

"You know you can just buy a bag of compost at the garden store, right?" his dad asked.

"I *know*," said Sam, who really wished people would quit asking him questions he already knew the answers to.

Sam turned to Annabelle. "But even if I buy compost, it's for Rudy to live in. It's not to compost Rudy in."

"Um, Sam?" Annabelle looked at Sam as though she felt sorry for him. Sam wondered why.

And then Sam got it.

If Sam put Rudy in dirt, then Rudy

would get mushy and turn into dirt.

Dirt would not save Rudy. Not even really good dirt.

"Maybe I should just put Rudy in the freezer," Sam said.

"And then what?" Annabelle asked.

"Buy him a hat?" Sam said. "And maybe a scarf?"

"I think you need to prepare yourself for reality, Sam," Annabelle said. "But who knows? Maybe rutabagas last longer than other vegetables. You and Rudy might have months left together."

"Could we look it up?" Sam asked his sister.

Annabelle nodded. "After dinner. We'll sit on the couch and look it up."

After dinner, Annabelle and Sam sat on the couch and looked it up.

There was good news, and there was bad news.

The good news was that rutabagas could last for four or five months in a root cellar.

The bad news was that Sam didn't have a root cellar.

Rudy would probably last four or five months in the refrigerator, Sam thought, but what kind of life was that?

Sam knew that Rudy would probably be happiest living in dirt, even if he ended up getting mushy. Sam would do everything he could to give Rudy the best dirt possible. And maybe instead of getting mushy, Rudy would figure out how to stay firm. Rudy seemed like a pretty smart rutabaga to Sam.

But even if Rudy could stay firm, there

was more bad news. Sam realized later when he took Rudy out of his backpack. Rudy's face was starting to wear off. When Sam tried to fix it using a ballpoint pen, he didn't do a very good job. Now Rudy looked like he had a headache.

"He looks cranky like Mr. Stockfish," Annabelle said when Sam walked across the hallway to show her Rudy. He was hoping Annabelle could use her marker to make him look happy again.

Annabelle got out her red marker and drew over the line Sam had drawn with the ballpoint pen. The problem was, the ballpoint pen had dug into Rudy's skin. So even when Annabelle marked over it, it just looked like a frowning face with a red lipstick smile.

"I'm sorry, Sam," she said, handing

Rudy over. "I think you're going to have to live with Rudy's new look."

Having an angry-looking rutabaga in his backpack was not as much fun as having a rutabaga that smiled at him like it enjoyed his company.

Sam put Rudy back in his backpack.

Who knew that having a rutabaga for a friend could make your life so complicated?

Chapter Nine

The Most Expensive Poop in the Store

On Saturday Sam's dad drove Sam to the garden supply store to buy a bag of compost. It would be months before the leaves and potatoes in his compost bin turned into actual compost. He couldn't wait that long. Rudy needed the best dirt possible immediately.

There were several types of compost to choose from. There was compost made from chicken manure, and compost made from cow manure. There was also compost made from mushrooms, and compost made from worm poop.

"I would like to get the worm poop compost," Sam told his dad, even though the worm poop compost was more expensive than the other kinds. Sam guessed you'd need about five hundred worms pooping night and day to make enough for even a small bag. Were there worm poop farms? he wondered. If there were, he'd like to visit one.

"Why the worm poop, Sam the Man?" his dad asked.

"Because it's the funniest," Sam

said. "Maybe it will cheer Rudy up."

After they put the bag of worm poop compost in their car, Sam and his dad went to the other side of the store and found posts and chicken wire to make a compost bin. Then they drove to Mrs. Kerner's house. When they got there Sam's dad pulled a post digger out of the trunk of the car.

"We need to dig four holes," he explained to Sam as they walked to the backyard. "Then you'll hold a post in a hole, and I'll shovel dirt into it and stomp it down. Once we have all four posts in, I'll staple chicken wire around them, and there you have a compost bin!"

An hour later the compost bin was done. Sam shoveled in all the manure from the manure pile. He put in the scraps he'd been saving in his big bucket. Then he used a pitchfork to stir everything around.

Sam thought his compost bin looked cool. He hoped the scraps and straw and manure turned into dirt fast. He wanted Rudy to enjoy it.

Sam would like to see a smile on Rudy's face again one day.

After lunch Sam went out to the garage and found an old box. With his dad's help he filled the box with the worm poop compost, and then he dug a hole in it. He took Rudy out of his backpack and placed him face-side up in the hole.

"This box is your new home," he told Rudy. "I think it will make your headache go away."

"You know rutabagas don't really get headaches, right, Sam the Man?" his dad asked.

"They *might* get headaches," Sam said. "We don't actually know if they do or not."

"They might, if they actually had heads," his dad said.

Sam guessed his dad was right. Rudy might have a face, and his face made him look like he had a head. But he didn't have a head. He didn't have a brain. He didn't even have a face, not a real one.

Maybe Sam had been wrong to try to be friends with a rutabaga.

"Do you want me to go with you to pick up your compost scraps?" his dad asked after Sam had patted down the dirt so that Rudy was covered. "I could pull the wagon."

"No, thanks," Sam said. "Mr. Stockfish is going with me. He gets cranky if he doesn't get his daily walk."

Today was the third day Sam had collected compost scraps from his neighbors. He hadn't gotten many on Thursday, but on Friday, Stella Montgomery made a carrot cake, so she had lots of carrot peels to put in Sam's bucket.

Mr. Stockfish was waiting by his mailbox when Sam got to his house. He looked fancier than usual. He was wearing a tie, and his black shoes were shiny.

"You know Mrs. Kerner's birthday isn't until next week, right?" Sam asked. "You look dressed up."

"I'm perfectly aware of when the party is," Mr. Stockfish said. "This is how I always dress. Well, maybe not the tie."

"Or the shiny shoes," Sam pointed out. "And you smell good, too. I mean, nicer than usual. I'm not saying that you usually smell bad."

"I put on aftershave," Mr. Stockfish said. He sniffed the air a couple of times, like he also thought he smelled good. "I always put on aftershave on Saturdays."

The first two neighbors had left their vegetable scrap buckets by the front door. All Sam had to do was dump their small buckets into his big bucket. There were potato peels and moldy bread and apple cores and broccoli stems all mixed together. When they got to Mrs. Kerner's yard, Sam would shake them all out on top of the pile and then cover them up with the straw from the chicken coop

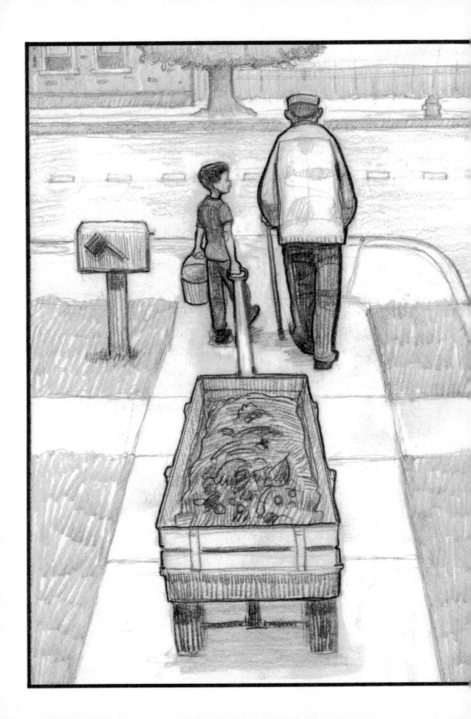

and leaves from Mrs. Kerner's yard.

"I think you should knock on the door this time," Sam said when they reached Stella Montgomery's house. "I bet Mrs. Montgomery would like the way you smell."

Mr. Stockfish straightened out his tie. "You're probably right," he said. "She would. But I don't want to give her the wrong impression."

"Like what?" Sam asked.

"That I splashed on extra aftershave for her benefit," Mr. Stockfish said.

"Who did you splash it on for, then?" Sam asked.

Mr. Stockfish's cheeks grew red. "It's none of your beeswax who."

When they got to Mrs. Kerner's house, the driveway was empty.

"I wonder where she's off to," Mr.

Stockfish said. He sounded disappointed.

Sam looked at Mr. Stockfish. He looked at his tie and his shiny shoes. He took another sniff of Mr. Stockfish's aftershave, which smelled like Christmas trees.

He remembered Mr. Stockfish and Mrs. Kerner sitting in the lawn chairs, holding their chickens. He remembered how Mr. Stockfish wasn't frowning.

"I bet she'll be home soon," Sam said. "She can smell your aftershave then."

"Harrumph," growled Mr. Stockfish. But he didn't frown, and his eyebrows didn't make an angry *V* between his eyes.

It was the happiest Sam had ever seen him.

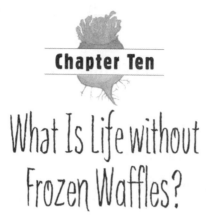

Chapter Ten

What Is Life without Frozen Waffles?

Sam hated going shopping after school. He liked his regular after-school plan best. He walked home from the bus stop, ate two frozen waffles that were still frozen, and then picked up Mr. Stockfish for their daily walk to see their chickens. This was the perfect plan as far as Sam was concerned.

On Monday it turned out his mom had a whole different plan in mind.

"I e-mailed Mr. Pell that I'm going to pick you up after school today," she said at breakfast. "Don't forget and get on the bus."

"Why are you picking me up?" Sam asked, feeling disappointed. He loved taking the bus. There were no seat belts, and sometimes Miss Louise, their bus driver, sang in a loud silly voice that made Sam and Gavin crack up. Once, Gavin rolled out of the seat and into the aisle, and Miss Louise had to pull the bus over until he calmed down.

"You have a birthday party to plan for," Sam's mom said.

Sam was confused. His birthday wasn't until May.

"Mrs. Kerner's birthday party, remember?" Annabelle said in a loud whisper.

"Oh! I printed out the instructions for charades from the Internet yesterday," Sam told them proudly. "And I thought maybe we could go to the store on Friday and buy some cupcakes. If they don't have sprinkles, we can add some."

Sam's mom shook her head. "There's a lot more to planning a party than that, Sam the Man."

"And store-bought cupcakes never taste as good as they look," Annabelle added.

So here it was Monday afternoon, when Sam should happily be eating his frozen waffles, but instead he was at the store listening to his mom and Annabelle argue over the best color for party streamers.

"Sam, you should choose," Annabelle said. She held up a package of green streamers and a package of blue ones. "Me, I like the blue."

"Green is more festive," Sam's mom said.

"Blue is everybody's favorite color," Annabelle said.

Sam sighed. He reached up on the shelf and pulled down one package of white streamers and one package of red. "These will match the cupcakes," he said.

Sam's mom and Annabelle agreed that this was a good point. "Now let's pick out some plastic tablecloths," his mom said.

"Plastic's bad for the environment, Mom," Annabelle pointed out.

"This is getting too complicated," Sam said.

They got napkins that said "Happy Birthday!" instead. It wasn't until they were in the checkout line that Sam read the words "Now You're Three!" on the back.

"She's a lot older than three," Sam said, showing his mom.

"I think these napkins could confuse a lot of people," Annabelle said.

Sam's mom suddenly looked very tired. She took the napkins out of the cart and hid them behind the gum rack. "I think I have plain white paper napkins at home," she said. "We can use those."

"Or Kleenex," Sam pointed out. "Which would come in handy if anyone's allergic to chickens and has to sneeze a lot."

On their way home, Sam looked at everything they'd bought for the party. He looked at the birthday party plates and the birthday party hats. He looked at the streamers and the candles and the red sprinkles and white frosting and the silver foil cupcake liners and the boxes of yellow cake mix.

It seemed like a lot of stuff for a party where only four people were coming, five if Gavin got back from soccer on time.

Sam leaned forward. "Does anyone know what Authors is? Mrs. Kerner says she wants to play Authors at her party."

Annabelle held up her phone from the front seat. "Meet me on the couch when we get home," she said. "We'll look it up."

"Why can't we look it up now?" Sam asked.

"Because I'm reading about bees," Annabelle said. "I'm thinking about getting a hive of bees for our backyard."

"You should stop thinking about that,"

Sam's mom said. Her voice sounded like a rubber band that had been pulled as far as it could be pulled without snapping.

Annabelle opened her mouth and then closed it. She turned to Sam. "I'll go ahead and look up Authors now."

Sam nodded. He thought that was a good plan.

"It's a card game," Annabelle said after a minute. "And all the authors are really old."

"We could draw their pictures on index cards," Sam said.

"Or we could print out pictures from the Internet and tape them to real playing cards," Annabelle said.

"We've got at least three packs of cards in the junk drawer," Sam's mom said. She sounded happier now that Annabelle had stopped talking about bees. "You could use one of those."

Sam patted his mom on the shoulder. "Good plan!"

"Yeah, Mom," Annabelle said. "Thanks."

Sam's mom smiled at Sam in the rearview mirror. "So are Dad and I invited to this party?" she asked.

"Sure," Sam said. "You could even carry the cupcakes over to Mrs. Kerner's house."

Sam leaned back and counted. If his mom and dad came, and if Gavin got back from soccer on time, there would be seven people at the party. Eight, if you counted Mrs. Kerner. Sam didn't know whether to be excited or really nervous. Maybe agreeing to have a party for Mrs. Kerner hadn't been such a great idea.

Don't forget, he reminded himself. You're doing this for Rudy.

Sam took a deep breath and let it out. He had forgotten about Rudy and the compost pile. He forgot there was a reason for the streamers and the party hat and the red sprinkles and vanilla icing and not getting to eat his frozen waffles right after school.

Having a reason made it all worthwhile.

Chapter Eleven

Say Good-Bye to Your Vegetable

They had less than one week left of their vegetable unit in science. This was probably a good thing, Sam thought at school on Wednesday. Even Gavin's new carrots looked old, and Will's head of cabbage had lost most of its leaves.

Caitlyn's potato still looked okay, and so did Marja's eggplant, but Caitlyn and Marja never took them out of their cubbies anymore. They didn't take them on walks at recess like they had the first week of the vegetable unit.

Next Monday the class was going to start a unit on the solar system. People were already talking about what planet they wanted to do their reports on. It was like their vegetables had never existed.

"I hope you have enjoyed this science unit," Mr. Pell said when everyone in Room 11 had put their lunches in their cubbies and hung their backpacks on their hooks and had taken their seats and stopped their talking.

"I think we've learned a lot," he went on. "We have learned about how things grow and how important the vitamins we get from vegetables are and why plants need rain. What else have we learned?"

Emily raised her hand. "We've learned

how our bodies digest vegetables."

"Very good," Mr. Pell said. "What else?"

"That some vegetables get rotten faster than others," Rashid said.

Mr. Pell nodded. "That's true. Anything else?"

Sam looked around. No one raised their hands. He didn't know if he should say what he wanted to say. What if it was dumb?

He thought about Rudy in his house of compost—compost that Sam had spent his hard-earned money to buy. He thought about the compost bin in Mrs. Kerner's yard, where microbes and bacteria were slowly turning potato skins and carrot peels into dirt.

He thought about the smile on Rudy's face.

Sam raised his hand. Mr. Pell pointed at him. "Yes, Sam?"

"I learned that vegetables are our friends," Sam said. "Even if they get rotten. All you have to do is put them in a pile, and sooner or later, they'll make more dirt. And then you can grow more vegetables to eat."

"An excellent point, Sam!"

"We should make our own pile," Marja said. "My mom said that when we're done with our vegetable unit, I should just throw my eggplant away."

"Mine too," said Caitlyn.

"Mine too," said Will.

"No fair," Emily complained. "I already ate my green bean!"

"I already ate, like, ten of mine," Gavin said. "But I still have a few more."

"I think making a compost pile with our vegetables is a great idea," said Mr. Pell. "I wonder where we could put it."

Sam looked around the room. He saw a lot of excited faces. He saw a bunch of people who had old and tired vegetables that needed a good home.

He raised his hand again.

"Yes, Sam?" Mr. Pell said.

"I have a plan," said Sam.

Chapter Twelve

Sam the Man and the Rutabaga Plan

On his way to Mrs. Kerner's birthday party, Sam stopped by his garage and picked up Rudy's box. Rudy was going to the party too.

"You'll have fun," he promised as he carried Rudy's box across the street to Mr. Stockfish's house. "There'll be chickens and cupcakes and lots of other vegetables for you to talk to."

Sam had decided to think of the compost

bin in Mrs. Kerner's backyard as an apartment building for vegetables of all shapes and sizes. A broccoli crown might live in one apartment, and next door might be a family of potato peels. Every couple of days things got stirred around, and the broccoli crown and the potato peels found themselves in new apartments with new neighbors. It seemed to Sam like an exciting way to live.

He thought Rudy would enjoy it there.

Mr. Stockfish met Sam at the front door. He was wearing a tie for the second Saturday in a row, but this week he smelled more like a pumpkin pie than a Christmas tree.

"Did you bring the cupcakes?" Mr. Stockfish asked Sam.

"My mom's bringing them," Sam said.

"I took over the games this morning."

"Did you decorate the way we talked about?"

Sam nodded. This morning Sam had hung the red-and-white streamers from the chicken coop, and he and Annabelle had strung blue-and-white lights in several of the trees near the deck. The chickens had clucked happily when they'd turned the lights on.

"Decorations make all the difference at a party," Mr. Stockfish said. He patted his pocket. "Okay, I've got my present. Let's get moving."

When they got to Mrs. Kerner's house, Gavin, Emily, and Rashid were waiting for them in the driveway. They each had a present in one hand, and a paper bag in the other.

"What do you have in the box, Sam?" Emily asked. "Is that your present for Mrs. Kerner?"

"No, the party is my present," Sam said. "This box is where my rutabaga lives."

Gavin ran over to Sam. "Can I see the worm poop? Does it stink?"

"It doesn't have any smell at all, and it just looks like dirt," Sam said. "But you can look if you want."

"It makes sense that it looks like dirt," Gavin said as he peered into the box. "Worms eat dirt, right? So they probably poop dirt, too."

"Worms eat a lot of things," Mr. Stockfish told Gavin. "Not just dirt. You should study vermiculture."

Gavin looked confused. "I should study worm-a-culture?"

"No, *verm*—" Mr. Stockfish shook his head. "Forget it. Let's go around back."

They all followed Mr. Stockfish into Mrs. Kerner's backyard. A bunch of people were there, including Mr. Pell and most of the other kids from Room 11, Sam's parents, Francine the mail carrier, Curtis the grocery store's bag boy, and Annabelle. The chickens were clucking loudly and bumping into one another inside the coop. Sam could tell they were excited. He guessed this was their first party.

Mrs. Kerner was wearing a crown made out of aluminum foil. She looked more like a queen on her throne than just a regular person sitting in a deck chair. When she saw Sam she waved and called, "I can't believe how many people are at my birthday party!"

She pointed to her crown. "Your sister gave this to me for my birthday. I feel very royal."

"You're queen for a day!" Mr. Stockfish said. He walked up the steps to the deck and pulled a small white box from his pocket. "And every queen should have her chariot."

Mrs. Kerner took the lid off the box and looked inside. Her face lit up like a jack-o'-lantern. "Oh, Mr. Stockfish! How did you know?"

"What is it?" asked Sam. "Is it an actual chariot?"

"Yes, it is," Mrs. Kerner said. She showed Sam the box. "It is a Hot Wheels 1965 red Ford Mustang convertible. Exactly what I wanted!"

"I thought you wanted a real one," Sam said.

Mrs. Kerner shook her head. "I don't like to drive if I don't have to."

Sam felt disappointed. If he'd known Mrs. Kerner would be happy with a toy car, he would have gotten her one.

Mr. Stockfish put a hand on Sam's shoulder. "Don't worry about the car," he whispered. "This party is the best present. I bet your parents are proud of you."

Sam was pretty sure this was Mr. Stockfish's way of saying *he* was proud. But Sam pretended he didn't know that. He didn't want to make Mr. Stockfish grumpy on such a happy occasion.

"It's time to play charades," Annabelle announced. She had come up onto the deck and was standing next to Mrs.

Kerner's chair. "Everyone gather around, and I'll explain how."

Later, Sam had to admit that the students of Room 11 were not great at charades. He thought maybe charades wasn't the best game for second graders. To play charades you had to be good at counting the number of syllables in a word, and you had to remember that when someone said "little word," they meant "the" or "at," not "cat" or "pot."

They were also not the best at Authors. Authors had too many rules. But Mrs. Kerner, Mr. Stockfish, and the other adults seemed to enjoy playing Authors very much. So Sam and Gavin and the other kids from their class got cupcakes with vanilla frosting and red sprinkles and went to look at the chickens.

"Do all the chickens have names?" Caitlyn asked. "Because if they don't, you could name one after me."

"Or me," Marja added, and then everyone was saying, "Or me!"

"They all have names," Sam said, "so they can't be named after anyone."

"Could you name an egg after me?" Caitlyn asked.

"It will get eaten," Sam said.

"That's okay," Caitlyn said. "But could you make it a blue one?"

"Sure," said Sam.

After everyone finished their cupcakes, Emily said, "I think it's time to do our plan."

"But you don't have a vegetable anymore," Rashid reminded her.

Emily opened her paper bag and

pulled out a green bean. "I got a new one," she said. "I didn't want to be the only one who didn't contribute."

Everyone got their bags. Sam got his box. He led the way to the compost bin. "So, guys, this bin is full of leaves and vegetable peels and chicken manure," he said. "One day it will be dirt. But it won't be just any dirt. It will be the best kind of dirt to grow flowers and vegetables."

A few kids clapped.

"Now we are going to put in our vegetables from our science unit," Sam went on. "And next year we'll add the compost from this bin to our school garden. Who wants to go first?"

Emily raised her hand, but Gavin said, "You should go first, Sam. It was your idea."

Sam reached his hands into Rudy's box. It had been a week since he'd last seen Rudy, and now he was a little bit afraid. What if Rudy had gotten brown and mushy? What if he didn't look like a rutabaga anymore? Closing his eyes, Sam pulled Rudy out of the dirt. Keeping his eyes closed, he patted Rudy to see if he felt the same. He did! Sam smiled.

Emily gasped. "I can't believe it!"

Sam's eyes popped open. Was something wrong with Rudy?

He looked down at his hands.

What he saw was a rutabaga.

It was half purple and half yellow.

It was about the size of a softball, with a little brown stump on top.

It had green leaves growing out of its little brown stump.

It had green leaves growing out of its little brown stump?

It had green leaves growing out of its little brown stump!

"Rudy's still growing!" Sam shouted.

"Rudy's still growing?" Emily asked.

"You heard him!" Gavin yelled. "He's still growing!"

"I thought all our vegetables were dead," Will said.

"Not this one—this one's alive!" Sam said. He held Rudy up over his head, like he'd just been named Vegetable Champion of the World.

Now Sam wanted to show Rudy to someone who wasn't in second grade, someone who knew a thing or two about rutabagas.

He saw Annabelle standing by the chicken coop, talking to Leroy.

"Look at Rudy," Sam said, running over to her. "He's got leaves!"

Annabelle looked. "He sprouted," she said.

"So he's still growing, right?"

Annabelle nodded. "Looks that way. You should plant him in the school garden."

Sam thought about this. If he planted Rudy in the school garden, he could visit him every day at recess. Or at least he could visit his leaves, since most of Rudy would be underground. Which meant Rudy's face would be underground, and Rudy's face was Sam's favorite part of Rudy.

Only Rudy didn't really have a face, did he?

"You know what the most confusing thing about Rudy is?" Sam asked Annabelle.

113

"What?" Annabelle asked Sam.

"He's not actually a person. But I keep thinking he is. It's hard to make decisions about a vegetable when you think it's a person."

Annabelle nodded again. "I've noticed that. Once, Mom put a cherry tomato in my salad, and I named it Margaret. And then I couldn't eat it. Couldn't eat *her*."

"And you love cherry tomatoes," said Sam. "You always get extra when we go to a restaurant with a salad bar."

"I guess I just loved Margaret more," Annabelle said.

Sam thought for another minute.

"Do you think I should eat Rudy?" he asked when he was done thinking.

"No, I think that would be weird," Annabelle said. "I think you should grow him."

Sam thought so too. And when he told people he was going to look at the school garden, he'd say, "I'm going to see my rutabaga" instead of "I'm going to see Rudy."

He looked at Rudy with his new head of leaves. "You're okay being a vegetable and not a person, right?"

Rudy looked at Sam with his half smile, half frown. He didn't seem to hear what Sam was saying.

Maybe that was because he didn't have any ears.

Maybe that was because he was a rutabaga.

"But you'll always be *my* rutabaga," Sam told him. "And I'll always be happy we were friends."

"Come on, Sam. We're getting ready

to compost!" Gavin called from the other side of the yard.

Sam set his rutabaga down in the dirt next to the chicken coop. He—it—would like it there. Rutabagas liked dirt.

Especially rutabagas that still had some growing to do.

Acknowledgements

It takes a village to raise a rutabaga, and I deeply appreciate Caitlyn Dlouhy for making sure we didn't end up with turnips instead. Thanks also go to the marvelous Alex Borbolla, the supremely talented Amy June Bates, the divine book designer Sonia Chaghatzbanian, and star copyeditor Clare McGlade. As always, Justin Chanda is my hero.

A big tip of the hat to Sam's first big fan, Xyrell Goldston, star reader! Finally, big love to Clifton, Jack, and Will Dowell, and to Travis the dog, who keeps me company while I write.